NEVER
TAKE A PIG
TO LUNCH

and other funny poems about animals

Selected by STEPHANIE CALMENSON
Pictures by HILARY KNIGHT

DOUBLEDAY & COMPANY, INC., GARDEN CITY, NEW YORK

For o.f.m., with love

Library of Congress Cataloging in Publication Data
Main entry under title:
Never Take a Pig to Lunch.
Summary: A collection of humorous poetry
about animals by well-known poets.
1. Animals—Juvenile poetry. 2. Children's poetry,
American. 3. Children's poetry, English. [1. Animals—
Poetry. 2. Humorous poetry. 3. American poetry—
Collections. 4. English poetry—Collections]
I. Calmenson, Stephanie. II. Knight, Hilary.
III. Title
PS595.A5N4   811'.008'036
ISBN: 0-385-15592-1 Trade
ISBN: 0-385-15593-X Prebound
Library of Congress Catalog Card Number 80-2040
Copyright © 1982 by Stephanie Calmenson
Illustrations copyright © 1982 by Hilary Knight

For permission to reprint, grateful acknowledgment is made to:

Atheneum Publishers for "Flamingos" by Robert S. Oliver from CORNUCOPIA. Copyright © 1978 by Robert S. Oliver.

A. R. Beal, Literary Executor of the Estate of James Reeves, for "Cows" by James Reeves.

Dana W. Briggs for "Tip-toe Tail" by Dixie Willson, which originally appeared in *Child Life* magazine, 1924. Copyright 1924, © 1958 by Rand McNally & Company.

Lady Chaplin for a poem (called "Phyllis and Henry" in this volume) from the movie LIMELIGHT by Charles Chaplin. Copyright by The Roy Export Company Est.

Eileen Cole for "Daphne the Dinosaur."

Delacorte Press for three poems (called "Household Pets" in this volume) from POEMS FROM SHARON'S LUNCHBOX by Alice Gilbert. Copyright © 1972 Alice Gilbert.

Harper & Row, Publishers, Inc., for "Drats" from WHERE THE SIDEWALK ENDS by Shel Silverstein. Copyright © 1974 by Shel Silverstein.

Houghton Mifflin Company and The Macmillan Company of Canada Limited for "The Last Cry of the Damp Fly" from GARBAGE DELIGHT by Dennis Lee. Copyright © 1977 by Dennis Lee.

Pyke Johnson, Jr., for "The Toucan."

Jack Kent for "Puppies," which originally appeared in *Humpty Dumpty's Magazine*, October, 1967. Copyright © 1967 by Parents' Magazines Enterprises, Inc.

Alfred A. Knopf, Inc., and Gerald Duckworth & Company, Ltd., for "The Vulture" from CAUTIONARY VERSES by Hilaire Belloc, published 1941.

Alfred A. Knopf, Inc., for "Bees, Bothered by Bold Bears, Behave Badly" from THE COLLECTED POEMS OF FREDDY THE PIG by Walter R. Brooks, copyright 1953 by Walter R. Brooks; for "The Crybaby Cow" from THE BIRTHDAY COW by Eve Merriam, copyright © 1978 by Eve Merriam.

J. B. Lippincott, Publishers, for "I Wouldn't" from YOU READ TO ME, I'LL READ TO YOU by John Ciardi, copyright © 1962 by John Ciardi.

Little, Brown and Company for "The Ostrich" by Ogden Nash, which originally appeared in *The New Yorker*, copyright © 1956 by Ogden Nash; for "Notice" from FAR AND FEW by David McCord, copyright 1952 by David McCord.

Macmillan Publishing Company, Inc., for "Roosters" from POEMS by Elizabeth Coatsworth. Copyright © 1957 by Macmillan Publishing Co., Inc.

Pantheon Books, a Division of Random House, Inc., for a poem (called "Dog and Master" in this volume) from UNCLE EDDIE'S MOUSTACHE: TWELVE POEMS FOR CHILDREN by Bertolt Brecht, translated by Muriel Rukeyser. Copyright © 1974 by Stefan S. Brecht.

Susan M. Schmeltz for "Never Take a Pig to Lunch," which originally appeared in *Cricket* magazine, January, 1977. Copyright © 1977 Open Court Publishing Company.

Windmill Books for a poem (called "Bad Elephants" in this volume) from AN EYE FOR ELEPHANTS by William Steig. Copyright © 1970 by William Steig.

CONTENTS

RUFF
WAR HERE

NEVER TAKE A PIG TO LUNCH

Never take a pig to lunch
Don't invite him home for brunch
Cancel chances to be fed
Till you're certain he's well-bred.

Quiz him! Can he use a spoon?
Does his sipping sing a tune?
Will he slurp and burp and snuff
Till his gurgling makes you gruff?

Would he wrap a napkin 'round
Where the dribbled gravy's found?
Tidbits nibble? Doughnut dunk?
Spill his milk before it's drunk?

Root and snoot through soup du jour?
Can your appetite endure?
If his manners make you moan
Better let him lunch alone.

SUSAN M. SCHMELTZ

BAD ELEPHANTS

My mother gave me all she had
To see the elephants being bad:
They ran through town
And knocked things down
And threw spaghetti at Abigail Brown.
WILLIAM STEIG

ROW, ROW, ROW YOUR GOAT

Row, row, row your goat
Gently down the stream.
Merrily, merrily, merrily, merrily,
Life is just a scream.

STEPHANIE CALMENSON

NOTICE

I have a dog.
I had a cat.
I've got a frog
Inside my hat.

DAVID McCORD

THE KICKING MULE

My uncle had an old mule
His name was Simon Slick
'Bove anything I ever saw
Was how that mule could kick!

He kicked a feather from a goose
He pulverized a hog
He kicked up three old roosters
And swatted at a dog.

When I went to feed that old mule
He met me with a smile
He backed one ear and winked one eye
And kicked me half a mile!

ADAPTED BY
STEPHANIE CALMENSON
FROM AN AMERICAN
FOLK SONG

ROOSTERS

"Get out of my way!"
  says Rooster One.
"I won't!"
  says Rooster Two.
"You won't?"
"I won't!"
"You shall!"
"I shan't"
Cock cock a
doodle doo!

They pecked.
They kicked.
They fought for hours.
There was a great
to-do!
"You're a very fine fighter,"
  says Rooster One.
"You're right!"
  says Rooster Two.
    ELIZABETH COATSWORTH

FIGHT
TODAY

BEES, BOTHERED BY BOLD BEARS, BEHAVE BADLY

"Your honey or your life!" says the bold burglar bear,
As he climbs up the tree where the bees have their lair.
  "Burglars! Burglars!" The tree begins to hum.
    "Sharpen up your stings, brothers! Tighten up
      your wings, brothers!"
"Beat the alarm on the big brass drum!
  Watch yourself, bear, for
    here
      we
        come!"

Then the big black bees buzz out from their lair,
With sharp stings ready zoom down on the bear.
  "Ouch! Ouch! Ouch! Don't be so rough!"
    He slithers down the tree, squalling, "Hey let me
      be!" Bawling,
"Keep your old honey. Horrid sticky stuff!
  I'm going home, for
    I've
      had
        enough!"

WALTER R. BROOKS

13

I WOULDN'T

There's a mouse house
In the hall wall
With a small door
By the hall floor
Where the fat cat
Sits all day,
Sits that way
All day
Every day
Just to say,
"Come out and play"
To the nice mice
In the mouse house
In the hall wall
With the small door
By the hall floor.

And do they
Come out and play
When the fat cat
Asks them to?

Well, would you?
                    JOHN CIARDI

DRATS

Can anyone lend me
Two eighty-pound rats?
I want to rid my house of cats.
SHEL SILVERSTEIN

PHYLLIS AND HENRY

Walk up, walk up,
It's the greatest show on earth.
Walk up, walk up,
And get your money's worth.
See Phyllis and Henry
Those educated fleas,
Twisting and twirling
On the flying trapeze.
And any time you feel an itch
Don't scratch or make a fuss
You never can tell, you might destroy
Some budding genius.

CHARLIE CHAPLIN

DAPHNE THE DINOSAUR

Daphne the Dinosaur
Could not fit through her gate.
So Daphne decided
To lose a little weight.

For lunch, she ate just half a tree,
And drank just half a brook.
She went out jogging every day —
Oh, how the forest shook!

Daphne watched her diet,
And went for long hard runs
Till Daphne the Dinosaur
Weighed only twenty tons!
EILEEN COLE

COWS

Half the time they munched the grass,
   and all the time they lay
Down in the water-meadows,
   the lazy month of May.
     A-chewing
     A-mooing
To pass the hours away.

"Nice weather," said the brown cow.
   "Ah," said the white.
"Grass is very tasty."
   "Grass is all right."

Half the time they munched the grass,
   and all the time they lay
Down in the water-meadows,
   the lazy month of May.
     A-chewing
     A-mooing
To pass the hours away.

"Rain coming," said the brown cow.
   "Ah," said the white.
"Flies is very tiresome."
   "Flies bite."

Half the time they munched the grass,
   and all the time they lay
Down in the water-meadows,
   the lazy month of May.
     A-chewing
     A-mooing
To pass the hours away.

"Time to go," said the brown cow.
    "Ah," said the white.
"Nice chat." "Very pleasant."
    "Night." "Night."

Half the time they munched the grass,
    and all the time they lay
Down in the water-meadows,
    the lazy month of May.
        A-chewing
        A-mooing
To pass the hours away.
        JAMES REEVES

THE CRYBABY COW

Moo boo hoo
moo boo hoo
moo boo
moo boo
moo boo hoo
        EVE MERRIAM

TREE TOAD

A tree toad loved a she-toad
Who lived up in a tree.
He was a two-toed tree toad
But a three-toed toad was she.
The two-toed tree toad tried to win
The three-toed she-toad's heart,
For the two-toed tree toad loved the ground
That the three-toed tree toad trod.
But the two-toed tree toad tried in vain.
He couldn't please her whim.
From her tree toad bower
With her three-toed power
The she-toad vetoed him.

ADAPTED BY STEPHANIE CALMENSON,
                            AUTHOR UNKNOWN

FLAMINGOS

Ah-choo!
(I couldn't help it.)

In a furious flurry
Of flapping, flailing wings
The whole flock took flight
And fled frantically in all directions.

In the center of the silent swamp
I was left alone,
Blowing my nose.
    ROBERT S. OLIVER

HIPPOPOTAMUS

See the handsome hippopotamus,
Wading on the river-bottomus.
He goes everywhere he wishes
In pursuit of little fishes.
Cooks them in his cooking-potamus.
"My," fish say, "he eats a lot-of-us!"
RACHEL PHILLIPS

23

TIP-TOE TAIL

A fish took a notion
To come from his ocean
And take in the sights of the town.
So he bought him a hat
And a coat and cravat
And a one-legged trouser of brown!
  He did!
And a one-legged trouser of brown!

His suit fit so queerly
That everyone nearly
Went following out on the street!
But the best of it all
Was how handsome and tall
He could walk when he didn't have feet!
  He did!
He walked when he didn't have feet!

Now I must confess that
I surely would guess that
A fish trying walking would fail.
But with no one's advice
He looked perfectly nice
On the very tip-toe of his tail!
  He did!
On the very tip-toe of his tail!

DIXIE WILLSON

PUPPIES

There were puppies on the sofa
  And puppies on the chairs
And puppies in the vestibule
  And on the cellar stairs
There were cold ones on the icebox
  And hot ones near the stove
There were puppies by the pack and herd
  And puppies by the drove
There were puppies in the parlor
  And puppies in the hall
And puppies on the porch and roof
  And on the garden wall
There were puppies in the attic
  In the bedroom
In the den
  And even in the closets
There were puppies (nine or ten)
  "Look at all those puppies, Henry.
Aren't they just dear?"
  "Enjoy them while they're puppies, Jane.
They'll be full-grown dogs next year."

JACK KENT

THE VULTURE

The Vulture eats between his meals,
  And that's the reason why
He very, very rarely feels
  As well as you and I.

His eye is dull, his head is bald,
  His neck is growing thinner.
Oh! what a lesson for us all
  To only eat at dinner!
      HILAIRE BELLOC

DOG AND MASTER

A dog with a mouth that's much too small
Can hardly eat his dinner at all.
That makes his master a happy man,
Seeing the dog eat the little he can.
Full of meanness, food, and glee,
He says, "I've found the hound for me."

BERTOLT BRECHT,
TRANSLATED BY MURIEL RUKEYSER

THE LAST CRY OF THE DAMP FLY

Bitter batter boop!
I'm swimming in your soup.

Bitter batter bout:
Kindly get me out!

Bitter batter boon:
Not upon your spoon!

Bitter batter bum!
Now I'm in your tum!

DENNIS LEE

29

WHAT TO SEE..

AT THE ZOO

First I saw the white bear,
  Then I saw the black;
Then I saw the camel
  With a hump upon his back;
Then I saw the grey wolf,
  With mutton in his maw;
Then I saw a wombat
  Waddle in the straw;
Then I saw the elephant
  A-waving of his trunk;
Then I saw the monkeys—
  Mercy, how unpleasantly they—
Smelt!

WILLIAM MAKEPEACE THACKERAY

ZOO TRAIN

WOMBA

MONKEY

HOUSE

PEANUT

THE OSTRICH

The ostrich roams the great Sahara.
Its mouth is wide, its neck is narra.
It has such long and lofty legs,
I'm glad it sits to lay its eggs.

OGDEN NASH

THE TOUCAN

Of all the birds I know,
Few can
Boast of as big a bill as a
Toucan.
Yet I can think of one
Who can;
And if you think a while, too,
You can:
Another toucan in the
Zoo can.

PYKE JOHNSON, Jr.

OSTRICH

31

HOUSEHOLD PETS

There's a black sheep in the shower
Having a shampoo.
The water is so very cold
That he has turned bright blue.

There's a monkey in the bedroom
Jumping on the bed.
He's bouncing up so very high
The ceiling's touched his head.

There's a camel in the kitchen
Standing at the sink.
He's just crossed a sandy desert
And would like a nice cold drink.

ALICE GILBERT